The Dead Zone

Dr. Sommers is researching rituals of certain cults in Central America. He has made a lifetime study of the practices and keeps meticulous notes.

He is found at his desk. He was writing about an orchid used in certain rituals. It is said that the flower can be made, through certain incantations, to expand and cover the head of a person, thus smothering him.

He died of suffocation. He had also recently run afoul of certain of the medicine people who were involved in those rites.

Det. Lt. Osvaldo Quinteros Perez is called to investigate. He is a specialist in such cults. The place where this happened was in the part of the Indigeno territory he referred to as the dead zone. It is known for deaths connected to those cults.

His friend and fellow cop is Renaldo Estes. They are quite the team.

The Dead Zone

© 2013 & 2020 by C. D. Moulton

This is a work of fiction. Any resemblances to persons, living or dead, or to events is purely coincidental unless otherwise stated.

Contents

About the author

CD Moulton has traveled extensively over much of the world both in the music business, where he was a rock guitarist, songwriter and arranger and in an import/export business. He has been everything from a bar owner to auto salvage (junkyard) manager, longshoreman to high steel worker, orchid grower to landscaper, tropical fish farmer to commercial fisherman. He started writing books in 1983 and has published more than 350 books as of January 1, 2023. His most popular books to date are about research with orchids, though much of his science fiction and fantasy work has proven popular. He wrote the CD Grimes, PI series, and the Det. Nick Storie series, Clint Faraday series, and many other works.

He now resides in Gualaca, Chiriqui, Panamá, where he writes books, plays music with friends, does research with orchids and medicinal plants. He has lately become involved in fighting for the rights of the indigenous people, who are among his closest friends, and in fighting the extreme corruption in the courts and police in Panamá.

He offers the free e-book, *Fading Paradise*, that explains what he has been through because of the corruption.

CD is the discoverer of the Chadam Protocol for curing cancer.

Facebook page Ambrosia peruviana for cancer.

The Dead Zone

Exit Dr. Sommers

Marta Valdez opened the front door, and sighed. The Doctor, as they called Dr. Sommers, had fallen asleep at his desk in the den, again. She could see the light from under the door. He got so wrapped up in his work he sometimes did that.

She knocked and opened the heavy door. He was slumped across the desk. He didn't wake up, so she went to shake him.

What an odd color! Sort of purplish.

He was cold! He wasn't asleep, he was *dead*!

She choked back a scream, and ran to the sala for the phone there. She didn't really know who to call, so she called the police. They would send a man right over. The Doctor's doctor was Dr. Fernando Ramirez, so they'd wake him and bring him along. Probably a heart attack.

Officer Renaldo Estes looked over the scene, and shook his head. It didn't look right. It wasn't any heart attack.

He called the station and told them to send over

the CSI team. He felt it would be a good idea for them to do a complete. This didn't look natural. He'd seen a lot of bodies who died from natural causes in his twenty two years on the police force.

He was very careful to not touch anything. The computer was off, but the monitor was on. The little yellow light was on. There might be something there. One of the newer officers would have to check that. He knew how to file a report and to search the net with the computer, but that was all.

Dr. Ramirez soon came in to greet Aldo (as everyone called him), who pointed to the desk. Ramirez had no more than glanced at the body when he said, "Not heart. Something very odd. Possibly some kind of stroke ... but that doesn't seem right, either."

He moved closer, but didn't touch anything. He knew the CSI team would have to bring their own doctor, a qualified medical examiner, to make any declarations. Aldo told him they were on the way.

The team came in, so Aldo and Doc went to talk with Marta. She didn't know anything. She came to work, the same as always, the light was on in the den, Dr. Sommers sometimes went to sleep while he was working, she went in, he was dead.

"Has there been anyone who was having any kind of problems with Dr. Sommers?" Aldo asked.

"No ... well, that witch woman, and some of those kind of people didn't like him, because he was showing people most of what they did was just tricks."

"Witch woman?" Doc asked. "There are three or four here. Which one?"

"Well, all of them. They didn't like him telling people they were all fakes, and were just, what he called, 'ripping them off.'"

"What do you mean?"

"Well, like they would pay a dollar for the stuff for the skin. They make it from that plant in front the butterflies like so much. Lanterna or something. He says anyone can break up the leaves and soak them in rubbing alcohol for a few minutes and pour off the, what he called 'extractions'. Put it in body oil, like that cocoa butter stuff, and you have the same thing they charge a dollar for, but for ten cents. Like that. Like putting in lemon juice with it for parasites.

"You can't drink it. It's poison."

"Why would they ... oh. They don't pay the dollar anymore. You have to extract it and use it within a couple of days, so what they could make for a dollar would last a couple of months," Doc said. "A dollar every three days is ten dollars a month. He showed me that, and I've even told some people how to make and use it. I wouldn't charge for anything like that. The people here don't have the money."

"Yes," Marta replied. "They try to make him pay for what they can't sell anymore. He tell them to kiss his royal rusty ass. He say they are common ladrones and cholus."

Doctora Elvina Suarez came out to say he died of suffocation. They couldn't find how it was done, but were making as thorough a finding search as they had ever made. There were papers all over the desk about poisons the medicine men and witches made, and the spells they used.

She then went back inside. Doc went with her to check out what he could, then they took the body. Aldo oversaw the entire operation, and made a fast call to a friend in the police he had worked with a couple of times in the past. He was a specialist in the cults, and how they committed murders.

The computer specialist, Doug, came while he was on the phone with Osi (Det. Lt. Osvaldo Quinteros Perez). He studied the machine and checked what was there to check before turning it on. Aldo told him the monitor was on, so someone else had probably turned it off. Estevo Arcas, the computer expert, nodded, and watched the machine boot, stopping it at one early point to read the script that came onto the screen.

"There was something not yet saved when the computer was shut off. It's in the backup, so we can see what it was to the last time it made the backup file. Let's see what we have. It's in Word Perfect. Ahh!"

He brought the saved file to screen.:

The orchid, Ctsm. integerinum is used by certain tribes in the coastal areas as a death omen and method. It is said that the flower is made, with an established ritual, to cover a man's head, and can smother the victim quickly. I have had this process described by two people who had no contact with one another, one in Honduras, and one in Costa Rica. There were references made to the plant here in Panama' by Dr. Samosa and Dr. Lincoln. Dr. Samosa had seen the method worked, and saw the results. He reports that a man did die, and that it was by suffocation. He could not explain what had transpired, in that case. It was the event that drew his interest. He reported it in his initial essay, and is expanding it in his upcoming book as an unexplained case that he has found evidence of being a true manifestation of magic.

I have the specimen of the Cstm. oerstedii, which is the species that is used in most cases, as it is a very dark flower. A darker flower is a psychological point with several such rituals that seems to make the story more believable. The form of the flower is such that one might well imagine it covering one's head like the hood on a shroud.

My contact with various of the practitioners who use this, and there are very few, leave me with the suspicion that this is another of those things that are merely to scare people. The form of the flower suggests Father Death, so the stories were continued and expanded. The main data that forms this conclusion is from a

That was it. It seemed the computer was shut down at that moment.

"I wonder if this plant on the windowsill it the orchid he was describing," Aldo said. "I can see what he meant about the shroud! It looks like a man wearing a shroud!

"I've seen a lot of these plants. There are a couple growing on the trees in the parque. The Indios use them in folk medicine, somehow. They have a use for a lot of different things."

Osi came in, looked around the room, greeted everyone, and said, "So! Catch me up!"

"Read the screen, first. Maybe it'll give you a perspective," Doc suggested.

Osi read the screen, and said he'd heard of that, but it wasn't one of the things that were used often. Very few knew the rituals, or whatever.

"Is that the kind of plant?" Aldo asked, pointing to the big plant on the windowsill. Osi went to inspect it.

"Hmm. This is getting a bit scary," Osi finally said. "I wish I knew more about the ritual and the expected results. I can gather the victim died by suffocation?" Doc nodded.

"This plant has three stems of flowers. There are four flowers per stem, but one is missing from the middle stem.

"Did you find that flower anywhere? he asked with great trepidation."

"Uh-oh?" Doc answered. "Yes. It was on the desk, actually, oh, shit! On his head!

"Come on! It's two inches across! It couldn't smother him on his nose, much less cover his whole damned head!"

"That's what ... this is a ritual, one of the four, that Dr. Ames couldn't find an answer for. He saw it worked, twice. He was right there. He couldn't explain it!"

"He saw the flower grow enough to where it could cover a head?" Aldo asked.

"No. He saw the ritual, and saw the dead body. He had medical training, and said there was no question the victim died of suffocation. There was no one else present in the place at the time."

"I'm not going to start believing in witchcraft

murders!" Aldo said, stubbornly. "There's an explanation that makes sense. We have to find it!"

"I most sincerely hope we can do just that," Osi replied.

"What can we do?" Doc asked.

"Nothing yet. We have to have something to go on. See if anyone saw or heard anyone around here since ... eleven thirty last night. That backup was made at eleven fifty two, so we have a pretty accurate time of death, I think.

"My worry is that no one was here."

"Someone was obviously here," Aldo replied.

"They were?"

"The computer didn't turn itself off at eleven fifty two last night, or any other night."

Osi laughed. "I would have thought of that, but maybe not until sometime next week. I'm a little more relieved by that. I just have to hope there's no way for a spell to turn off a computer.

"I did think of another thing."

"What?"

"The computer would turn off if the current was broken. The monitor would go to standby, the way you found it. Someone could have done that from outside."

"No. The breakers are inside, in this house."

"Another thing," Doug said. "There's a battery backup for the computer. It lasts for about three minutes. It's so the computer can save anything. This backup file was because the computer was turned off, not from any break in the current flow. If it had been that, the backup would state that the computer was shut down by an outside cause. Someone pushed that power button, right there. It stopped the current inside, past where the battery could kick in.

"See, there are two buttons on this one. There's also the regular click command. You...."

"So we know it was deliberately turned off, right here at the desk," Aldo said. "I won't begin to understand how you know that."

Doug laughed, and gave him the finger.

"I'll see what we can dig up about who may have been around at that time," Aldo said. "You can see what else is on the computer that may have anything to do with this. Osi can do whatever he does. We can meet at the station at four thirty to debrief?"

They all agreed to that.

Osi's Investigation

Osi went first into the cluttered bedroom and meticulously searched through everything there, finding nothing out of the ordinary.

Next, the bathroom. Nothing.

Next, the kitchen. If there was even suspicion of poisoning everything in it would be tested. For this, he merely checked everything over to be sure nothing smelled or looked different. The utensils were in place, and the drawers were in order. Marta was a good housekeeper. Only the bedroom and the desk in the den were messy. They were clean, but disordered.

The sala. Nothing.

The den, with Doug working with the computer, didn't show much, but he wasn't sure what he was looking for. Sommers had evidently kept thousands of things in stacks. When Osi checked, he found a loose kind of order. He didn't doubt Sommers could have gone instantly to whatever he needed.

Osi leafed through two piles of papers and photographs that caught his attention. They were concerned with investigating the witchcraft in

Panama'. He would box those stacks and anything else and take them home to study. He didn't doubt there was plenty to be found among them, but hadn't a clue as to where, other than those stacks.

He had things boxed and ready to carry out when he suddenly stopped. Doug asked him why he yelled that. He didn't have any memory of yelling anything.

"You said, 'With all those, where in *hell* is it?' Loud!"

"Doug, did he keep a lot of digital photos on that computer?"

"Oh! Right! I didn't see any camera, anywhere. He took a lot of pictures. He was good. It's a ... wait a minute. I'll check."

He went to the computer and put the arrow over a photo icon. The legend came up: 8:13PM, June 4, 2012, Nikon Sommers 2010.

"He took that picture at eight thirteen in the evening, the day before yesterday. The camera is a specially designed Nikon. I'll bet that thing cost him three grand!"

"But where is it?"

"I'd say your killer took it. I think it'll be a great giggle when he tries to sell it, or anything."

"It means we have to look over every photo we can find," Osi said slowly, thinking deeply. "The fact it was taken means there was something to do with it involved in this mess.

"Doug, please tell me he only took ten pictures, ever, and he labeled them 'clue one through clue ten.' I don't want to have to spend an hour going through five hundred photos that have nothing to do with anything!"

"No problem! There aren't any five hundred pics! There are four four gig memory sticks of them, closer to twenty five thousand!"

"I hate your damned guts!"

They laughed, as much as finding you're going to have to spend two full days looking at someone else's special photos can make you laugh. Osi figured, with those two boxes of data files and those pictures, he wouldn't be able to really start for more than a week!

"At least, he was interesting. I've read some of his notes. He has a writer's style that keeps your interest. He was maybe a little too careful and too deep into a subject, but it is interesting. He didn't believe most of it was actual magic, but he had serious questions about a few things. The orchid was one of them. That was what he was working on when he was croaked."

"And that flower was on his head."

"Yeah. Scares the shit out of a guy! Here's this genius with two Phd's who believes some of it's true magic, or psychic power, or something. You wonder if it would be too smart to catch whoever we're after!"

Osi shrugged. "It's what I do."

"It ain't what *I* do!"

That got him the finger.

Osi went back to the bedroom where he checked a few places more carefully that he'd gone over in a more superficial way when he searched earlier. There was no camera at all, much less a custom designed job.

The bathroom. Ditto.

There was a distached bodega out the back door. Aldo had checked, and said it was just garden tools and that kind of thing, and that there was no evidence anyone had been in it recently. Osi went to check it out, to find a pair of dirty overalls and rubber boots in a corner. There was a memory card from a camera in a pocket.

The overalls were slightly damp on the cuffs. They hadn't been there for long.

The camera had been used three days ago. What if he took more than one card of pictures? What if this was one that he changed wherever he was shooting the pics? The dampness would last three days on the cloth, because the bodega was closed and locked. The door sealed enough that there wouldn't be very much drying, inside. It had also rained during the night, three days ago and again last night.

Osi thought, trying to remember. Three nights ago. It had rained early, about one o'clock in the morning, but that would be the morning of three nights ago, not three days. It was four calendar days ago.

Osi suddenly wanted to know where Sommers was from the evening four days ago until 8:00PM three nights ago!

He went back inside. Doug was just finishing. He handed him the memory card. Doug inserted it into the reader. The legend said there were 987 pictures. Doug groaned, loudly, but Osi said they probably would only have to look at the last ten or twenty.

They were pictures of a few kids, then pictures of some hard to see scenes around a campfire.

"I can bring most of them out fairly well, I think. He had a camera that recorded in almost no light. It's a matter of brightening them to where we can see. He has one hell of a program for that, probably designed for use with that camera. Let's see."

He brought up a photoshop program, and loaded the last picture. He manipulated the light until they had a picture that wasn't very clear, but was detailed enough that they could see it was a man and woman, standing beside the fire. Their backs were to the fire, and details could be made out of their sides, but not direct. Doug said it was because the fire backlighted, and they didn't have any reflection in front. You could see enough of the side of the woman's face to see she was a black with shiny hair to her shoulders. She had a diamond earring that was fairly distinctive. The cop in Osi said that earring could maybe identify her. Doug nodded.

They went back on the card, and were able to see enough in some pictures to identify individuals. Two of them were locals Osi had seen around the town. Then it was the kids. Sommers had seemed to concentrate on the kids with rounder faces and flatter noses. Osi knew a couple of them.

"He was tracing certain families back to Haiti, and even to Africa. They'd made a map for using DNA, somehow," Doug said. "I read a lot about that research. He had some pictures of those kids with stuff like that they had ancestors from China, as well as Africa. One family, that one with the straight reddish hair and sort of yellowish eyes, had ancestors from ancient Greece, or something. He made a joke, let's see, it was in ... this one, I think." He split the screen, and put a paper on, with a picture of Aaron, a local boy with dark black hair with reddish tints and brown/yellow eyes.

This is a child of nine years named Aaron Leones. He features the traits found in the G411GE family. There is definitely DNA from the same original source as charted from the remains found in Egypt (G411-25/E919+02) that was connected closely to the family of Paris Galopoliertes. That root family is supposedly of direct descendence of Helios. (Maybe we could have a direct descendent of Apollo here! Hah!) The family has not been in great numbers at anytime we can discover, but has always exhibited a very strong influence. An odd thing is that the traits are visible only in the male progeny. The only thing that shows in female progeny is an occasional lighter eye color. That the traits are, at least to a great extent, sex-linked, seems defined. The genetic dominance factors that now so clearly show...

Doug turned to Osi. "Well! That was the joke. A black descendant of Apollo, here in Panama', three thousand years later! He liked to say things like that." He laughed.

"It ain't funny! Damn! Sommers was a hell of a lot better scholar than I ever guessed, and I knew him enough to know he was 'way up there!

"What in *hell* did he find that ended up with him dead?!"

"That's your department. I find the shit, you

make something of it.

"You don't really believe that kid who always begs quarters off of me is a descendent of a Greek god, do you?"

"No. And yes, in an odd way. He's a descendant in a family who are *supposed* to be descended from Greek gods. Until I find how Sommers actually was killed, I'm about ready to believe anything.

"Doug, do you know his father and mother?"

"I talk to the father, sometimes. I'd noticed that his eyes are more dark hazel than dark brown, but it didn't mean much to me. The mixes here can show up in a lot of ways."

"I'm just wondering if maybe our Dr. Sommers made a joke about it, somebody checked it, and found it's true, and is building a cult around them being descendants of gods, as proven by DNA."

"It wouldn't surprise me."

"But that makes the puzzle harder. What could be the reason to kill Sommers, if that were the case? He would be the one person who could show that there was a scientific connection to a family who were reputed to be direct descendants of gods! It doesn't make any damned sense!"

"Maybe Sommers was going to tell them it's all bullshit. That it's only one of those things that science comes up with that only has meaning to science. There ... maybe not! He had another piece ... maybe because someone said something about it. It was further along, maybe this."

He read something, said that wasn't it, and went on. He finally said that he'd found it, and brought it to screen:

This story that the Leones are minor gods is just plain silly. I think I was able to explain to Aaron, who's really a good kid, that it is only a story, that to be descended from a god meant there had to be that god to be descended from. Apollo was a legendary god. That means he was a made-up god. He was made up to explain the way the sun seems to go around the Earth, not vice versa.

His father said I was taking away a dream. I said I was stopping a silly thing that would embarrass them all, later. The boy could enjoy the tale, but he mustn't actually believe such a thing. It was alright to say there was a story that he is a descendant of a god, but you trace the story back and find that we are all descendants of those same gods.

I find that people will desire to believe in the possibility of such things. I find that is of no harm, but to believe in more than that as a tiny possibility becomes a negative thing that can....

"We seem to have a little thing to investigate, but I'll have to figure which angle of approach. Is it because Sommers would dilute the possibility the Leones are gods, or because someone else wants to use the story, or because someone else fears Leones will take away his power over the people?"

"You do have something to investigate, now. Maybe you can find something in that mess or in the photos that will tie something to something else."

"I can give it the old college try!"

They packed up the things they were going to take with them, and headed for the station. They were already half an hour late, but Aldo would expect that. This was Panama'. No one was ever on time for anything here.

Aldo's Investigation

Aldo left the Sommers' house and went to the station to file what he had. He could then go into town to see what he could see. If Osi took much of this seriously, it really was scary. There were things he'd investigated that showed that it was more than possible someone had a mental power that could be dangerous.

He was *not* going to accept that that flower, no matter how weird it looked, could kill anybody. He knew that some flowers could kill, like the Chalice Flower, that contained a narcotic poison so strong a tiny piece could kill. That was a long way from a flower that could grow large enough to cover a man's head and smother him!

He noted that the Phd's who said they had observed the ritual didn't say it was what really happened, only that they couldn't explain what had happened.

This was a sort of crazy voodoo thing. He had three women who were supposed to be voodoo queens, or whatever. He got along with all of them, so could ask them about the flower. Maybe he could find something. He had no other trail to follow. Yet.

That black woman they called Mama Edna was a good bet, and was closest. He went in to greet her. She said she didn't have any feeling that any voodoo magic was used that close to her. It was somebody who was trying to cause the people who understood the nature of the world and the nature of people trouble. Somebody choked the doctor to death, and tried to make it look like a spirit killing.

"Who would know about the death flower thing, other than you?" Aldo asked.

"Death flower? What do you mean?"

He hinted that there seemed to be a death flower in the room, and that it had been used, but he couldn't say how. He didn't know the spell.

"A death flower that chokes a person? There's a death vine spell that will do that. Not a flower."

"No. It's an orchid that's supposed to be able to cut off the air, somehow."

"It isn't any spell I know."

He thanked her, and went to the south end of the little town. Most of the people there were Indios. Mabel was a supposed medicine woman. She knew of the orchid, but didn't think there was anyone here who knew the spell. She didn't have much faith in magic spells. They were mostly just word devices that held the recipes for certain medicines. The voodoo women made a ritual when they were overheard quoting the spells as they made the medicines. They used their own names for plants and animal parts. People who heard them thought they were magic spells. Abracadabra was because someone heard some witch mumble, "Abrir la cadaver," which means "Cut open the body."

That wasn't definite, but was the kind of thing that happened. Cut open a chicken or lizard, and quote the old text while you do it. Abracadabra.

Next was the other end of town. In what the police called the dead zone. Too many murders in the area. A black/French woman everyone was afraid of. They called her Mama Nani. He'd checked her ID when she was involved in some kind of argument over someone owing her a few hundred dollars. Nanette Lefleur Lopez. Black Panamanian/ Jamaican mother and French father. She was a dark, intense woman, a little overweight, but not extreme. The men here liked their women a little fat. Some liked them obese.

Mama Nani let him in, suspiciously. He said he only needed some information about the death flower curse. She answered there were fifty death flower curses, minimum. Which one.

"The orchid. That one that looks like a man wearing a shroud."

"Father Death orchid. Flowers is children of Father Death. Walk beside you when death be seekin'."

"I mean the spell that makes them smother a person."

"I done heard it. Back home in Jamaica. Ain't nobody herebouts know it. Maybe south end of Colombia."

"It was used on Dr. Sommers. Last night."

"No shit!?"

"It seems to be the only explanation for what we've found."

"You done scarin' Mama Nani! Ain't nobody herebouts got the power! Probably ain't nobody herebouts ever done heard of it! I only know 'cause when I was to Jamaica last to visit Abuela Mama Gina. She done got it that look like that one all over here and she tell me bout what 'tis. She big powerful, but she no know spell."

Aldo nodded, and thanked her. Among the local witches, she was the only one who was more than a medicine woman.

He was going to have to concentrate on any strangers in the close area, which meant very few likelihoods. A few people on boats. This was the edge of the comarca land. They didn't encourage tourists, or investors, or anyone else.

There were three seagoing sailboats that had

been anchored offshore for from two days to more than a month. The one from two days ago would leave soon. They didn't get along with the people here. They were snobs, which meant they would be treated like dirt, but would think all strangers were treated that way. It wasn't at all likely they would be involved, but that remained to be seen. Being an asshole made you guilty of being an asshole, nothing else – usually.

It also made anyone in a position to do so want to match the ass-holiness (is there such a word?). Aldo heard the man and his "Queen-of-the-world" wife denigrating the people here and the police department here because she left a cell phone on a table at a restaurant and it was gone when she went back for it, an hour later.

He was going to enjoy the excuse to bring them in for a few questions. He checked with the only other person around who might know anything, the herbal doctor, Javier. He said Dr. Sommers had asked him about it, but he couldn't give him any help. He had heard the story, but didn't put much stock in those things.

Aldo wasn't a cop who was unqualified for his position who had been put out in the middle of nowhere, where very little ever happened. He was more than qualified, and was here because he wanted to be. It was that, or look for another occupation. He didn't like cities, even a little bit. The same thing was true of Osi. They fit with the people here, and were effective. The CSI team was a local doctora and three people who wanted to learn the craft.

He went to the station to get a few papers, then got on the police boat to go to the first sailboat, the assholes. He called, and was told in no uncertain terms that he wasn't going aboard for any reason, and he could get the hell away from their boat right the hell now, or have a complaint lodged against him for harassment – was that *quite* clear?

He sighed, and climbed aboard. The man came out with a rifle pointed at him. He smirked, and said to put the damned thing down, and produce a permiso to have it in Panamanian waters, or he was going to serve ninety days for deadly weapon law infractions. He was threatening an officer of the law.

"Then you will show me a warrant that says you can come here and molest us!" the man snarled.

Aldo handed him the warrant, and said, "I don't really need one. This is not the states. You will now show me the permiso for that and any other weapons I may find aboard this vessel."

The man called, and the woman brought out the permisos for the rifle and a pistol.

"Put the gun away, and I'll not charge you for threatening a police officer, unless I find that to be expedient, later.

"I was only going to ask you a few questions, here, then let you go. Your over-reaction to my presence tells me you have something to hide, so you and your wife will now accompany me to the station, where we can consider it as an official questioning."

"I'm not about to go to any dirty police station! The very idea!" the woman spat.

"You will come to the police station, now, either on your own, or in handcuffs, such as we use, or physically carried, if that becomes necessary."

"Look, officer. We've had nothing but problems since we came here. These people hate us for no reason!" the man wailed.

"They have ample reason, and you could have left here at anytime. Please get in the boat. Don't make it necessary for me to use force. That will not be to your advantage, I can promise you."

They locked the cabin, and made remarks about how everything they own would be stolen by these thieves here. They got in the boat.

"I can check your identification on the way, if you wish to save time," Aldo said. They handed over their passports, and he wrote down what he needed. The woman sat stiff, and wouldn't look anywhere except straight ahead. The man did loosen up a bit, and asked, "What is the problem officer? Why are we involved?"

"There was a murder, Mr. Wallace. It was done in a manner that no one here could have done it. We have to investigate anyone not from here to know if they are involved."

"Murdered! *We* are not involved in any *murder*!" the woman screeched. "I have *never*!"

Aldo came into the dock, and tied the boat, then pointed to the little police station, across the road. When they were inside, Mrs. Wallace announced, "I will not answer one question until my lawyer's present!"

"Okay," Aldo replied. "You can contact your lawyer, and I'll hold questioning until that lawyer is present, though I also will inform you that you don't have that option here, legally. I'll wait in deference to the fact the laws are different where you came from.

"Does that include you, Mr. Wallace?"

"Well, you realize that we aren't used to being treated like criminals. I think it would be better to wait until our lawyer is here to give us counsel."

"Very well. Please place all personal items and anything else you're carrying into those manila envelopes. We will inventory all items as we place them."

"What is that for?" Mrs. Wallace demanded.

"When a person is incarcerated, he or she may not enter the cell with any such things," Aldo replied, casually. "I think that is the same in the states."

"*Incarcerated*?!" she squealed.

"Yes. Until your lawyer is present to represent you. You certainly couldn't have believed you could just walk out of here if your lawyer isn't present. That's ridiculous.

"You haven't contacted your lawyer yet? How long until he arrives?"

The Wallaces looked at each other. He caved in. "What do you want to know."

"Where were you last night from eight o'clock until four this morning, and can you prove it?"

"We were on the boat, after ten. We ate at that awful little ... at the restaurant across from the market," he replied. "Lots of people saw us there. We had a discussion about the amount of *grease* in the food! It's intolerable!"

"What did you have?" Aldo couldn't stop himself from asking.

"The fried shrimp and French fries," he replied.

"I see. You ordered deep fat fried food, then complained about the fact it was fried in grease. I suppose they will remember that!

"Did you see or talk to anyone after that?"

"Yes. That Amos character. The dirty old man who sits on the dock and tries to make you pay him to watch your boat."

"Amos is a fixture. He owns the dock and a lot of the boats around here. He's not dirty. None of these people are. The fact he wears old clothes doesn't make him dirty. One doesn't often wear a tuxedo to watch a fishing dock.

"He does note everything, so he can say you went to your boat at, did you say ten o'clock?"

"Yes. We didn't leave our boat after that until you came."

"He'll know that. He can see the boats anchored offshore. He knows when anyone comes and goes, here. The dock is the only place to come ashore, unless you want to try to tramp through those mangroves.

"We can go talk to him. If he says you were on your boat, you were on your boat. If he agrees I'll take you back to your boat.

"Understand that I can hold you here in a cell until your lawyer arrives, then can charge you with several things that would keep you in that cell six months."

"That's it?" Wallace asked.

"It? Yes."

"But ... I thought, the way you treated us, we would be asked all kinds of questions about crazy things we can't even guess ... that it would be harder. We could have told you this on the boat!"

"Yes. You could have cooperated, and would be back to whatever you were doing in ten minutes. You have to realize that I merely reacted to the way you treated me. If you can't see something so obvious, I can predict that you'll have trouble everywhere you go."

They didn't say much more. Aldo took them to Amos's house. He said they didn't go anywhere, other than their boat. He took them back to the boat. Wallace actually broke down enough to say, "Thank you, Officer."

He went to the next boat. Alvin Wright and his girlfriend of the moment, Gilda Candinas, a girl from Dolega, a small town near David. They had stayed on the boat. Two friends, Carlos Chayos and his girlfriend, were with them until about two.

Aldo left the boat in the ten minutes he told Wallace it would have taken, and went to the third boat. He was about to tie to it when he saw the juju hanging over the cabin door.

The dinghy wasn't there, so the boat's owner was probably in the puebla. Aldo headed back to the little station. He was going to investigate the papers they had on that one, very thoroughly!

Very thoroughly, indeed!

Jujus

George Raymond Hanley, 32, from Tarpon Springs, Florida, USA. Construction contractor. Living in Panama' as a permanent resident, with investor's status. No record. Had a driver's license. Owned four properties, two on islands in the Caribbean, one on an island in the Pacific, and one on the mainland, near Alanje, a small town near David. Owned a four wheel drive Mitsubishi and a Ho Fai motorcycle. Surfer.

Aldo slid the paper across the desk to Osi, who read it over. He sat back, and said, "So?"

"I take pictures of everything," Aldo answered, showing Osi his digital camera. "Here's a picture of that juju on zoom." He located the picture, and passed the camera to Osi.

"Hmm. Bamboo? On a boat?"

"You see. That juju is for protection of a house made of bamboo, with a palm frond roof. That means Georgie Boy doesn't know anything about jujus, or that he stole that one somewhere. No witch would make that for a boat."

"You said he has two pieces of land with houses on them."

"Alanje? Bamboo and fronds? Isla Popa?"

"I see. It's not the kind of thing that was made here, either. Where else has he been, according to his passport?"

"It's a new passport. He's only used it here and in Belize. Belize is possible for that kind of juju, but not likely.

"I want to know where he's been in the United States. I want to know if he was ever around Dr. Sommers, there."

Osi nodded, and connected to the web with the desk computer there. "We fight ancient witchcraft with a modern computer!" he said, as he did a Google search on Hanley. He took twenty minutes to narrow it down to the correct Hanley.

"He was a minor partner with Jefferson and Thomas Construction in Houston, Texas. They did jobs in Louisiana, so he could damned well have met Sommers, there. He could have learned a little about jujus there, too."

"A little knowledge is a dangerous thing," Aldo agreed. "He learned about jujus, in general, but not about how specific a given one must be.

"He's on several blogs. He's a member of AOS, so that's another connection with the case."

"It is?"

"AOS. American Orchid Society. Give me the motive, and we've got a case, but I tend to think it would be a case against the wrong person."

"You do? Why?"

"Jefferson and Thomas? You gotta ask?"

"That occurred to me. It still doesn't rule anyone out. CIA uses those methods. WP might have him there because of something exactly like this."

"Whatever, we don't need him here. Have you ever met him?" Aldo sighed as he said it.

"Yes, I think so. Sort of longish hair, and a surfer's build. Great shape that can be caused by the surfing. Handsome, in a way, I suppose. The women like him."

"Want to go out there with me?"

"Don't see why not."

They got up and went to the boat and out to Hanley's sloop. He was laying in a hammock on the deck. When they came up and hailed him, he asked if he might use the head right quick, then he'd talk with them.

"We don't give a shit about drugs, unless you're selling or transporting in bulk," Aldo said. He laughed, and said to come aboard.

They tied, and went aboard. Hanley invited them inside, where they sat at the galley table with cold beers. Hanley said, "Okay. What?"

"WP or other?" Aldo asked.

"Other, but not what you think. How did you glom?"

"Jefferson and Thomas? You gotta ask?" Osi answered, getting another laugh.

"Yeah. Real original and clever. Difference is, it was."

"You ever actually been in Louisiana?" Aldo asked.

"I've never been on the mainland US, at all. Drop me off at the office address in Houston, and I'd be totally lost."

"Why Doc Sommers?"

"I swear, that wasn't us! We were protecting him. Our surveillance crap didn't catch anyone going in there. I'm beginning to believe it really was voodoo. I've seen some hair-curling things!"

"Give us some background."

"Doc Sommers was an independent scientist working for a university group. They're ground-breakers in the paranormal things. They take a lot of stuff that they know is paranormal and try to work out how and why. It almost always comes up with trickery, poison, hypnotism, or highly suggestible people. It was Doc's theory that the suggestible people were the key to the things that actually worked. Someone made the wrong suggestion to one of them, he tried it, it worked. He then retains an ability to use it. It's psychic power, of some sort.

"I watched as a Russian girl made a ping-pong

ball bounce all around inside of a bell jar that was pumped to a hard vacuum. She could point to a compass, and the needle would go crazy. She could do it, but didn't know how.

"Doc observed, and theorized she could cause a directed magnetic field with her mind. We argued that it would explain the compass, but not the ping-pong ball. He argued that it would, because the ball contained air, thus oxygen. The vacuum was an excellent dielectric. The magnetic field would form with the oxygen in the ball, it would charge and discharge, making the ball move to those charges.

"It sounded silly, so we made a thing where we could induce a magnetic field that would affect the oxygen in the ball. We were able to make the ball roll a little, but not much else. A magnetic field wouldn't work. Not one that small.

"He said try it with a maser. She was able to direct the magnetism. That worked exactly the way he said with the ping-pong ball *and* with the compass.

"His theory was that all the phenomena worked in a like fashion. He pretty well proved it. It didn't take a thing away from the simple fact that some people have a psy power.

"He turned to other things that were observed scientifically that couldn't be reproduced, proven, or disproved with science. That got him deep into the voodoo bit. There were several things that seemed to work that couldn't, the way he saw it, be from that kind of psy power. It had to be a much greater power.

"You see, he theorized that such a mind could use the power in a mind it reached to form a hard illusion, inside of that mind, that something was happening. We know about the Catholic Bleeders at Easter, and we know that mood will make a sickness worse or better. I should say, 'Mood and belief,' not just mood.

"He said the mind believed it was being starved of blood, so the circulatory system would stop the flow of blood to the brain. It's been shown pretty definitely that it's the kind of thing that does happen. It's behind psychosomatic responses."

"Psychosomatic diseases can be cured when the subject is convinced that's what it was," Osi pointed out. "Sommers would know, for fact, that's what it was. It wouldn't work on him."

"Which is why we know it was a physical murder, not a mental murder," Aldo said. "Either way, it was a murder. We might not have a hope of convicting a mental murderer, but we damned well can convict a physical one!"

"I have a problem," Hanley said. "Is my job a done failure, or do I stay on?"

"If you're not suspected as being what you are you might be in a position to help us," Osi said. "Was that juju out there on purpose?"

"I don't know what you mean."

"Where did you get it?"

"A magic woman in Belize. She said it would protect me from having anyone steal things from the boat."

"So she knew it was for a boat?"

"Sure! Why?"

"I wonder if that thing figures into this mess. It just might. I don't know ... let me bring a witch out here to answer some questions about that one little item that's out of place?" Aldo suggested. Osi looked questioning. Hanley shrugged. They talked about other things for awhile, then Osi and Aldo went ashore. Osi went to the station to look up some references Hanley had given them. Aldo went to call on Mama Nani. She agreed to try to read the juju. She said she would know right away if it had any power directed at it.

Cops and Witches

"This is Mama Nani," Aldo introduced. Hanley said he had met her, and welcomed them aboard.

"That juju is tellin' somebody somewhere all what you do or say where it can hear," she stated, positively. "It be a long way away, but it be close."

"Belize?"

"Yah. Maybe. An here, too."

"We have a killer being directed by someone in Belize," Aldo suggested.

"They ain't be no zombie here."

"No. This is coldblooded murder. I just have to find the motive, and I'll find the killer.

"Mama Nani, is there someone here who can ... I don't know how to say it. Communicate with someone in Belize without ... anybody can! Cell phones! Shit!"

"Mon, you better get rid of that thing out there! It be tellin' too much. It don't know me, and it don't have no power, but it do tell all. You get that thing away afore you gets on no cell phone. It can't hear me in here, but it can hear anything what's on a cell phone!"

"How do we get rid of it in a way the receiver won't know?" Hanley asked.

"It hear. It don't see. Like this here!"

She stepped outside, and said, "You watches what you do with that thing! You gonna set a fire, Mon!

"Hey! What that? A voodoo doll! What for you got that thing? Who's it affectin'?"

She waved at Hanley, and motioned for him to talk. "Oh, it's a thing I picked up in Jamaica, or somewhere. It doesn't affect anybody."

"They's s'posed to affect somebody. Gimme that. Who yells is who it affects!"

She lit a butane cigarette lighter, and held it under the Juju. It caught fire, and she waited a few seconds until it was totally in flames. "It dead. I hopes the one what make it be true connected! Real hotfoot, Charlie!

"Now, you use the cell phone."

"If someone's using a cell phone, I can find out in two minutes," Hanley said. He went back to the computer, and slipped a memory stick into a USB port. He called up some kind of program, and inserted a complicated code. After a minute, a line appeared on the screen. He held down [Alt] and added a code. The screen scrolled to a long list of numbers. He punched 011, which Aldo knew was Panama', then another, then a third. One number was on the screen with a >4< after it.

"That number was called in Belize four times in the past forty eight hours. It came from this one, right here. That's the only one from this relay."

A cellular number was on the screen.

Aldo called the number. When it was answered he asked, "Quien habla?" That is common in Panama'. If you answer the phone in the USA and someone asks who's speaking, you hang up. In Panama', it's expected.

"Pasame a Gloria."

"Desculpame." He rang off. "So. I know who's calling from here. The time was barely within bounds. Now we have to figure how he did it, and if he was helped."

They went back outside, where the juju was a smoking piece of dry ash. There was a mini-transmitter cell phone board in the ashes.

"It wasn't voodoo. It was a regular type bug," Hanley said. "That brings up a question or two, by itself!"

There wasn't any denying that little fact! It was a professional type of thing. Someone was using the voodoo to cover what was certain to be something else, entirely.

Aldo and Mama Nani went back ashore. Aldo gave Mama Nani two dollars and a half for the "consultation" fee.

He didn't want to act too soon. He still didn't have motive, though he could get a conviction with what he had. He wanted to know who the real killer behind this was.

When Aldo had delivered Mama Nani home and returned to the office, he called Osi, who said he would be over in a little while. He was just finishing a set of notes.

"Anything new?" he asked.

"I know who killed him. I don't have a motive, and there's a direct connection somewhere else. I don't want to act precipitously."

"It wasn't voodoo?"

"I never thought it was, directly. It might be, indirectly. It can be one of those things where you can say it wasn't voodoo that killed him, but it was voodoo that made the killer kill him.

"Something else occurs to me. Why wasn't that number from the bug phone master on the relay tower?"

"Now you lost me?"

"I have to check. I may have found a way the killer can get away with it. I hope not."

He hung up, and called Hanley. "Why wasn't that bug on the relay numbers list?"

"Because it's being relayed from someone right here to the satellite, direct. I'm checking that, now. It could be from one other thing I know about."

"The military open relay lines?"

"They're not actual lines. They're circuits in the satellite. That was my choice."

"So it really is something some government is interested in, would you say?"

"I'd say something like that. Yes."

"Who do you work for, Mr. Hanley?"

"Call me George. I swear to you it's not something you would be against. We're trying to stop this kind of thing. It's a group that started out with the conspiracy theory, and found some things that are a hell of a lot deeper than that. It's not some government agency. We just use things that will make anyone who's checking think they're checking on another agency, thus the Jefferson and Thomas bit. You have to admit the first thing you thought was CIA. Second, WP. Two things that don't interest the people we don't want interested."

"I don't know who I can trust, anymore. I know who killed Sommers, I just don't know why. I don't see how it could be any government agency, while I don't see how it couldn't."

"Aldo, have you considered what Mama Nani said about cell phones? We're using them, right now."

"Yes. I use several. I bought them when I was in

David off a street vender. They're what you call throwaway phones. You don't see any caller ID on calls from them. My regular police phone always shows that."

"So they would have to be monitoring mine to know anything. I think maybe I'll get a couple of throwaways. If they're listening to this, learn what you can, now. By this time tomorrow, you won't be able to."

"Yes, they will."

"What ... oh. They only have one or two using that relay."

"There are more than that, but not many."

"Well, we can write, if there's anything we don't want known."

"I don't say anything I don't want known. What someone else says can tell me a lot."

"Uh-huh. Somebody knows something you said that only someone listening would know."

They chatted a bit longer. Aldo wasn't sure he could trust George completely, but he was sure he could trust him to a point.

He sat back to think. He needed motive for killing Dr. Sommers. That was critical, for some reason he didn't know. He just knew it was.

Okay. Sommers had found something about a voodoo curse. It was something that put someone in ... he must be slipping! He kept looking for a motive for killing Sommers, but he should have been looking for a motive for killing Sommers *in that way*! The method outweighed the motive, in this case – and he thought he just might know how! The method was the message.

What did that change?

As for his part, nothing. His part was to expose and prosecute a killer.

He thought more. He had to add all the known facts together. What Dr. Sommers had written was damned important, but he didn't quite know why. It was a nag at the back of his mind. What did Sommers find that threatened someone, in what way? Who? How?

Everything they had was right there on the computer. He was going to bring it up, and was going to find what his mind was hiding from him.

He read the excerpts from Sommers. He was on the third long treatise when he stopped. He went back to the first, and read it carefully. This had to be it, this had to be who, this had to be why. He had it all, but he didn't stand a least small chance of proving a thing.

He left the treatise on the screen, and sat back again. He had to formulate an approach.

Maybe he could do that!

He started a Google search, then did a Yahoo! search. It was more than possible. The second made it two hundred percent more likely he had this one figured right. The person behind it was untouchable, so long as that person stayed where claiming voodoo would have a case laughed out of court. No extradition.

So! The way to handle that was to have that person come to Panama' to help the police in the investigation.

He thought about it, again. He had to be right. It would be a matter of making a very small change, make an excerption, on a treatise that was right there on the screen.

Aldo went back to the computer, and was on it at four the next morning. He had read and studied more than three hundred pages of research notes and exchanges between Dr. Sommers and six other people. The more he read, the closer he got to knowing this was a finished case. All it needed was the arresting of the killer and the killer's sponsor.

He looked at the clock, showed great surprise, and went to lay on the ratty old sofa. The next thing he knew, Florence was shaking him awake. It was nine, and the two regular officers were getting to work.

He felt exceptionally rested. He called Osi and Hanley, then went to his apartment to clean up and get ready for the day. He was going to have an interesting day, he was sure.

He was going to contact some people with an offer and a request. If things worked out ten percent as well as he hoped, it would work.

He had a good breakfast, and went to the office at eleven. Osi was there, working, and Hanley came in a few minutes later. He explained that he was going to try to get the killer's sponsor there so he could arrest him.

He called Florence in, and said to arrest Carlos Chayos, and bring him in.

"What are the charges?" she asked.

"Murder. Take Salvatore with you, in case he gets bravo."

She left. Osi asked how he figured it.

"He was out at the Wright boat. He left at two. His girlfriend was with him. He got her drunk, or something, or maybe took her home, we can ask Wright if they were drinking, and went from out there to Sommer's place and came up from the beach. He would know where the alarms and such were, killed Sommers with some kind of device that smothered him, the flower was dropped on his head, Chayos went home, we have the rest.

"Okay. We know about that. You're probably right, but the killer's sponsor, as you call him, is in Belize. We still don't know who he works with. Maybe we can trace when we identify him, positively. I think it's damned important to know who this was for."

"It was for him. I have to make a couple of e-mail requests. If we can get him here, we can prove the rest of it fairly easily. Let's put it together, then I'll want to do something with one of Sommers' papers."

He went to the computer to send two e-mails, then brought the treatise to screen and made a copy. He took a part of it out, nodded, and saved it.

The phone rang. He answered. The caller ID had an unfamiliar number on it.

"Yes?"

"Officer Renaldo Estes, please. Lincoln calling here."

"Speaking."

"I just received an e-mail requesting that I aid you in the investigation of a dear colleague, Dr. Sommers. I was shocked to hear he is dead. I will help in any way I can. You stated it seemed to be a voodoo curse that killed him? That you can't find any other explanation?"

"Yes, Doctor Lincoln. We found references to his contacting you about this very method. We hope you can help us sort the mess out."

"I will come there, immediately! Dr. Sommers is a great loss to science! If you will have a way for me to reach you when I am in Panama' City?"

"I'll have a helicopter to bring you directly here. You can't know how deeply I appreciate this cooperation! I had hoped you could spend the time to e-mail me some information, but this is wonderful!"

"This thing you described has intrigued me for years. I will come as quickly as I can get a flight."

Aldo hung up, and smirked, then shook his head.

"I don't get the connection!" Osi cried.

The phone rang. Another unfamiliar number.

"Renaldo Estes."

"Dr. Enrique Samosa here. I just got your e-mail. I can't quite make any sense of it, but you say Sommers is dead through some kind of voodoo curse? The Death Flower thing?

"We were researching that project together. We couldn't find any way to refute it. Fascinating!

"How can I help? Is much disturbed? Would it be of use for me to investigate on my ... well, obviously! It was exactly what we were researching. I will come there. It is part of the research, so the grant will pay. I will arrive in David at six. You can arrange for me to come to you?"

"Yes, Dr. Samosa. I'll have a helicopter bring you directly here from the airport ... no. It will be too dark for the chopper, tonight. You will stay in the Hotel Nacional. I'll have a room reserved at our expense. You can come in the morning, as soon as there is sufficient light."

He soon hung up, and smirked again.

"Which one?" Hanley asked.

"The one who already had a flight booked when he got the e-mail," Aldo replied. "Shall we put this together?

"I really didn't expect Lincoln would come, but he may be useful. We have to be certain he can't communicate with Chayos."

"Handled," Osi replied.

"Let's make this one a smooth one," Aldo said. They nodded at that.

Finishing the Case

Samosa came roaring into the station like a runaway bull, giving orders that he was to be granted full access to all information, and was to be taken to the scene of the crime, immediately, if not yesterday or the day before! Nothing must be disturbed! Nothing!

"Dr. Samosa? I'm Aldo Estes. Please have a seat where we can go over what we have. The CSI team was thorough, and all the evidence is photographed, saved, sealed, and labeled.

"We must not get in too much of a hurry with this case. Things are missed, that way.

"Dr. Lincoln will be here in about two hours. We can go over his notes and photos – you might find something that means something. You will know references we can't hope to understand. We can go to the scene together. Nothing has been disturbed more than absolutely necessary, but we have photos that are very good, you will find. Nothing was missed.

"I read what he was writing, at the time of his death. The computer was turned off, but that program keeps timed backups. We don't know what he may have written after the backup. He had it run every five minutes, so there probably wasn't anything critical.

"He specifically mentioned you in that backup, so we contacted you."

"Hmm. Mentioned me?"

"Yes. He said you were a researcher who had made a very concise and detailed study, that you couldn't find a refutation of the curse deaths. I can bring it to screen where you can read it."

"Yes, yes! I will want that!"

"It's on this one, I think. Yes S one twenty." Aldo put the memory stick in the computer, and brought up the treatise. It was the same as they'd found, with a little bit cut from the end.

Dr. Samosa and Dr. Lincoln. Dr. Samosa had seen the method worked and saw the results. He reports that a man did die and that it was by suffocation. He could not explain what had transpired in that case. It was the event that drew his interest. He reported it in his initial essay and is expanding it in his upcoming book as an unexplained case that he has found evidence of being a true manifestation of magic.

I have the specimen of the Cstm. oerstedii, which is the species that is used in most cases as it is a very dark flower. A darker flower is a psychological point with several such rituals that seems to make the story more believable. The form of the flower is such that one might well imagine it covering one's head like the hood on a shroud.

My contact with various of the practitioners who use this, and there are very few, leave me with

"I have seen a report much like this. I know he ended it with being left with no way to refute it as being in the realms of true magic. We both tried every way we could think of to refute it. These kinds of things are usually fairly easy to show as trickery or something, but there are those two cases. Maybe another one here. Possibly there is no refutation. I have found a couple of things, not on quite this order, that aren't refutable. I believe I wrote about them. He refers to that here. It wasn't saved past that point, so we don't know what he was left with."

"This will be another one, unless we can somehow show that it was done through trickery, that smacks of actually magical powers – which are psy powers. That is what we were researching. We have found a *very few* cases where there seems to be a slight psy ability. This is a case of massive ability, and will prove my studies that indicate there is that ability in a selective few *Homo sapiens* that must be studied to any extent possible.

"You see, if there is that ability, anywhere, the military sciences in various places will want to compete to find its mechanism and those who can use it. Funding for university research, such as ours, is pitiful. Military funding, sad to say, seems unlimited. A grant of ten thousand dollars for the university study, ten million for military. Yes, it's totally disgusting and sickening, but that's the way of the world!

"I am compiling a book about this very thing. This will, if we are truly unable to refute it, place me into that military research area. It's one hell of a sad and disgusting thing to contemplate, but that's the sick world we live in.

"Now! We do have to get this right! We must not miss the tiniest detail, the tiniest possibility that it was not that ability! We can't overlook anything at all!

"If there is a killer here, he must be found. We must ascertain that it was done with that psy ability, and not through trickery or deceit! Show me all you have on this, and I will study it closely. It is possible Sommers found a discrepancy, and someone wishes that it not be brought forward. If it is there, I will bring it forward! If I can locate something, Dr. Lincoln is the most qualified man in the world to help me show it is whatever it is, and not another distraction or trick!

"Is everything here on this flash drive?"

"Yes. The entire case was put on that one so you and Dr. Lincoln could find, as you say, any discrepancies," Osi replied. "I've been on this so long I'm blurry. I don't really know what to look for. I'll leave it to you and Lincoln, and get a bite of breakfast, then go home to sack out for a month or so!"

"Yes, yes. I will study this carefully. Let me know when Lincoln gets here. We can discuss anything I can find, as to merit."

"We'll all use a little sustenance to advantage," Aldo said. "Can we bring you anything before we go?"

"No. Fine. Maybe coffee?"

They left. At the restaurant, Osi said, "He wants to find anything that can stop him from getting a ten million dollar grant, and erase it, would you say?"

"Pretty much exactly. I felt he would come to do exactly that. Leave nothing to chance. If he finds anything negative, he can get the world's second most learned person in the method to decide on its merit – which it won't have any of."

They chatted a bit more. Lincoln came in, and they put the two men together to discuss what they had. Samosa said they wouldn't need to view the scene. The pictures hadn't missed one millimeter of that house or room. He would request that he be allowed to use some of them in his book.

They would meet at five. They should be able to go through the important things, by then. They should be able to say definitely if it was or was not done through the voodoo curse.

Aldo was going to have a little surprise waiting at that meeting! He told them he felt that they would be able to say exactly how it was done, curse or other. There would be little room for doubt, after that meeting, and he would feel secure in releasing their findings, whatever they were.

He was going home for a couple of hours. He needed the rest. Osi and Hanley were ready. The surprise witness was ready.

Mama Nani was ready.

"Well, if you've made your complete study, we can finish this up tonight. I have other cases where I need to investigate a lot more deeply than this. We're lucky, in that we have people in the area who can help us with most things," Aldo declared."We have Osi for these psycho things, I'll turn it over to him now."

"That's psychic things," Samosa corrected.

"In a lot of ways," Osi said. "Like Aldo stated, we have people with abilities in different fields, right here.

"What I'll want to do first is bring up a short treatise by Dr. Sommers about the abilities of the locals. It was only two pages. What we want is the second page."

He selected a file on the memory stick, and brought it to screen. He amplified it enough that those a couple of feet away could read it

to the fact that these abilities are always among us, if in small ways.

i.e. There is a medicine woman on the camarca just east of here, Matilde, who is known to know when a woman is pregnant. She knows the sex of the child and what it will be named. She is never wrong, according to almost everyone in the area. A very famous man was here with his wife and she announced the woman was pregnant, that it was a girl, that its name would be Nicole. The baby was born exactly 268 days later.

That is but one instance. What we seek is not a known ability in a specialized area, it is a more massive talent.

A woman called Mama Nani here has an ability that may be based on fear and not an ability. No one can lie to her. She can make them tell things they are not aware they know. This warrants more study. We must find the mechanism to learn if it can, indeed, become a strong force.

"Mama Nani will be here momentarily to demonstrate her talent," Osi said, when they had read the page. "We also have a person who our modern DNA science tells us was at the scene of the murder. He has no explanation for having ever been there, and denies he ever was. DNA doesn't lie. The match is one hundred percent.

"Here's Mama Nani, now." He introduced her around. She stared at Samosa for a few long seconds. He was suddenly nervous. Samosa researched these things, and had stated, various times, that he had found specialized psy powers in a small number of people. Mama Nani looked like a witch, if a sort of pretty one.

"You deceitful, Mon!" she charged at Somosa, then went to sit in a chair. "What you want me here for, Osi. You no deceitful, ever. You want Mama Nani to say if he liar?"

"It wasn't why we asked you here, Mama Nani. It's good to know, but he's just a scientist who's studying psychic phenomena," Osi replied. He went to the interoffice intercom unit, and said, "Salvatore? Please bring Sr. Chayos in here."

Samosa jerked, but showed no further reaction. Chayos was led in and seated.

"What you done, mon? You don't lie none to Mama Nani or you soul rot in hell!"

"Mama Nani, I didn't mean ... I had to ... it was

because I couldn't stop! Honest!"

She stared in his eyes, and he slumped. "You done had you mind taken before! Who did it?"

He mumbled something. "A cel number? What? You tell Mama Nani an she help you."

He gave the cell number that called Samosa in Belize. Samosa was sweating. She suddenly spun on Lincoln, shook her head twice, and turned to Samosa. Her eyes rolled back, and she made a little dance. He looked like he would faint.

Mama Nani's voice seemed to be coming from somewhere else, and had a hollow ringing tone. Her lips didn't move.

"You done it! Tell them! or you soul rot in hell!"

Samosa did faint. He came to in a few seconds, to find Mama Nani a foot in front of his face. The look on her face was scary, even to Aldo, Osi, and Hanley.

"You goin' tell me all! Don't lie none to Mama Nani! You soul you don't believe you got rot in hell!"

"It was the money!" Samosa squealed.

"Tell all! Now!"

"I ... it was with a government man who was in Panama' when I was studying the medicine women on the Cuna Yala. He was there, and was an expert at post-hypnotic suggestion. We talked. He found what I was investigating, and said we could both get richer than Midas. We could get ten million dollars, unlimited expense accounts, and anything else we wanted, if we could only convince a panel that such a power was here. It was a panel that wanted to be convinced. That was why he was sent.

"We came here to speak with Sommers. He would never agree to subterfuge, and we knew it. We only convinced him to concentrate on the death orchid thing because it was a case I knew would never be resolved, and that could have been a real thing.

"I knew immediately that Sommers was very suspicious if some person we called 'Sergeant' was behind the research. I could see he suddenly had serious doubts about the ability.

"That is the saddest thing. It may be a true set of events. The Death Orchid ritual may be fact.

"I knew Sommers would research it too deeply, and with a belief it was false. He would find ways to guarantee it would be looked on with great suspicion, or even stark disbelief, by other serious researchers. I saw the ten million dollars evaporating.

"Quite by accident, we met this man, Chayos. He had been in a fight, and had stabbed a man. We saved the man and Da ... my contact, said he was a rather violent person, by nature, but a highly suggestible one.

"You see, you can't hypnotize a person to the point where he will do a thing he wouldn't do. Chayos is a natural killer type.

"He was to call me at anytime Dr. Sommers said anything that would indicate he was going to publish a negative major paper. He called. I used a phrase. We finished the conversation, and he did what the government man taught him. I don't know the entire thing, but it's some kind of pressure point that paralyzes a person, and you can simply smother them with your hand, or whatever.

"Now he's dead, and this research will ensure that the ability won't be considered for any grant. It's damned sad. We still don't know if it's a real talent."

"You tell we who this man is!" Mama Nani ordered. "You tell Mama Nani now!"

"All I know is that he's called Sergeant Danny, and that he represents the English, that's to say British, government."

That was a bit of a shock to all of them, but they managed not to show it. They thought they were talking about the US government, all along!

"Belize. I guess so," Osi said. "I think that will tie this case up tight. Thanks, Mama Nani."

"I did that one good, huh? Mama Nani can

maybe be a movie star!"

"It was an *act*?!" Samosa screeched. Lincoln was wide-eyed.

"Oh, Mama Nani knowed you was lyin' an is deceitful. I no can send you soul to rot in no hell. You got to do that youself."

"The power of suggestion. You believed it, it happened. If you'd have simply not answered, we couldn't prove a thing," Aldo said.

"I don't really think the testimony of a witch will carry any weight in court," Samosa snarled.

"Maybe not where you're from," Osi replied. "This place, in case you ain't noticed, ain't where you're from.

"Salvatore, please escort Dr. Samosa to a cell, and process him.

"Chayos, you can go. We have proof that you weren't acting in your right mind. I doubt it will be very long before you're dead, or in prison for life. It's part of you. That Sergeant Danny creep saw that, and used it.

"Well! Shall we break this one up?"

"If I might," Dr. Lincoln said. "May I have copies of Dr. Sommers' research? I will want to continue it. This doesn't really affect the truth behind the Death Orchid ritual, you know."

They looked around at each other. Osi nodded.

That was the truth of the matter: they didn't

know the truth.

C. D. Moulton's works are available on most major outlets as printed or e-books. CD writes the CD Grimes, PI mysteries, the Det. Lt. Nick Storie mysteries, the Clint Faraday mysteries, the Flight of the Maita science fiction series, books on orchid culture and many others of many types. Mystery, adventure, intrigue, science fiction, fantasy, para-normal, mild erotica, and factual.

Milton Keynes UK
Ingram Content Group UK Ltd.
UKHW020727080424
440801UK00013B/603